THE RAUCOUS AUK

THE RAUCOUS AUK
A Menagerie of Poems

MARY ANN HOBERMAN
ILLUSTRATED BY JOSEPH LOW 1911-

The Viking Press   New York

FIRST EDITION

Text copyright © 1973 by Mary Ann Hoberman
Illustrations copyright © 1973 by Joseph Low
First published in 1973 by The Viking Press, Inc.
625 Madison Avenue, New York, N.Y. 10022
Published simultaneously in Canada by
The Macmillan Company of Canada Limited
Library of Congress catalog card number: 73–5140

SBN 670-58848-2   *811   American poetry*

1   2   3   4   5   77   76   75   74   73   PRINTED IN U.S.A.

Where in the world are the animals from?
From where in the world do the animals come?
Why in the world do they live where they do?
Where do they live when they're not in the zoo?

They come from all over. No matter how hot
Or cold a place is, something lives in that spot.
(It may be a mere little worm of small worth,
But someone's alive everywhere on the earth.)

They live where it suits them, which often depends
On whether their neighbors are foes or are friends
And whether the food supply's fit for their feed
And whether the weather's the weather they need.

Some are quite fussy and only can thrive
In a special location, while others survive
In a number of places; and then there are those
Who seem to live everywhere anyone goes.

Where in the world are the animals from?
From where in the world do the animals come?
Why in the world do they live where they do?
Where do they live when they're not in the zoo?

BANDICOOT

The bandicoot
Is fond of fruit.
Australia's where she's found.
She likes to dig up gardens there
And burrow in the ground.
>   *How sandy for the bandicoot.*

The bandicoot
(Who dotes on fruit)
Is fond of insects, too.
She has a pouch
To hold her young
Just like the kangaroo.
>   *How handy for the bandicoot.*

The pouch is on her belly.
It closes on the top
And opens on the bottom
But the babies never drop.
>   *How dandy for the bandicoot.*

PYTHONS

The thick black pythons
Are braided tight together.
How do they untwine?

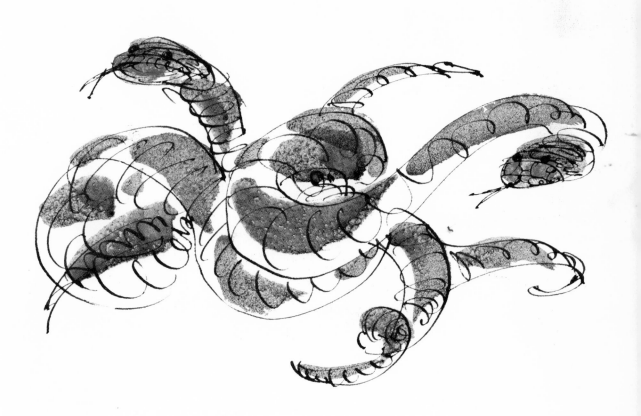

WHALE

A whale is stout about the middle,
He is stout about the ends,
& so is all his family
& so are all his friends.

He's pleased that he's enormous,
He's happy he weighs tons,
& so are all his daughters
& so are all his sons.

He eats when he is hungry
Each kind of food he wants,
& so do all his uncles
& so do all his aunts.

He doesn't mind his blubber,
He doesn't mind his creases,
& neither do his nephews
& neither do his nieces.

You may find him chubby,
You may find him fat,
But he would disagree with you:
He likes himself like that.

AUK TALK

The raucous auk must squawk to talk.
The squawk auks squawk to talk goes

AUK

ZOOGEOGRAPHY

Tigers live in India
Lions live in Africa
Alaska has the grizzly bear
      But bats and rats live everywhere.

Camels like it where it's hot
Polar bears prefer it cold
In the middle suits the hare
      But bats and rats live everywhere.

They live in both Americas,
Australia, Asia, too,
In Europe and in Africa;
The only ones who do.*

Otters like it where it's wet
Ocelots prefer it dry
Wolves and weasels do not care
      But bats and rats live everywhere.

*Except for me and you.

PROCYONIDAE

If you give a little whistle,
You might meet a cacomistle,
A coati or olingo
Or a raccoon with a ring-o;
I can name them by the dozens
And all of them are cousins
              And they're all related to the giant panda!

The kinkajou's another
That is practically a brother
To coatis and olingos
And to raccoons with their ring-os;
And every single one of them
Is different, that's the fun of them
              Yet every one's related to the panda!

Now they all have different faces
And they live in different places
And they all have different sizes,
Different noses, different eyeses;
But the family name for all of them
Is just the same for all of them
              And each one is related to the panda!

Raccoon

Kinkajou

Panda

GIRAFFES

I like them.
Ask me why.
　　Because they hold their heads so high.
　　Because their necks stretch to the sky.
　　Because they're quiet, calm, and shy.
　　Because they run so fast they fly.
　　Because their eyes are velvet brown.
　　Because their coats are spotted tan.
　　Because they eat the tops of trees.
　　Because their legs have knobby knees.
　　Because
　　Because
　　Because. That's why
I like giraffes.

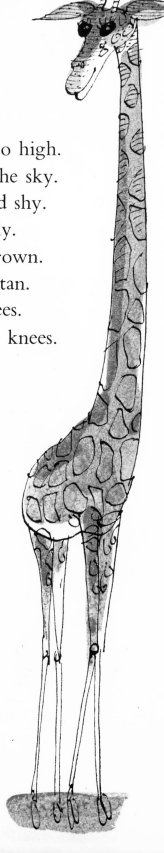

CAMEL

The camel has a heavy bump
                                        upon his back.
                It's called a hump.

Although it weighs him down, he moves

                                        with perfect grace

                upon his hooves.

ALLIGATOR / CROCODILE

The crocodile
Has a crooked smile.
The alligator's smile is straighter.

Or maybe it's the other way.
(With crocodiles it's hard to say.)

Perhaps the opposite is true.
(It's hard with alligators, too.)

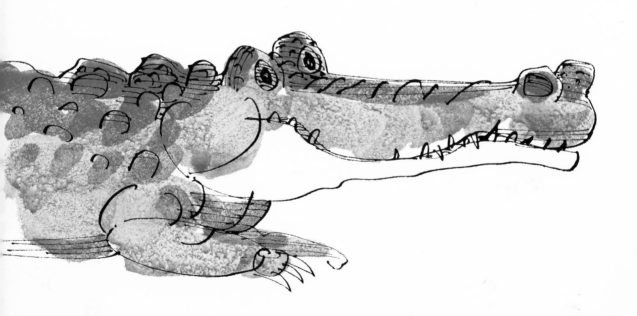

But if I write what I just said,
The first way might be right instead.

And then again the second might
As easily be wrong as right.

Or right as wrong. Likewise the first.
In that case should they be reversed?

Or left alone? Or should I switch?
I can't remember which is which!

The crocodile
Has a crooked smile?
The alligator's smile is straighter?

FOXES

A litter of little black foxes. And later
A litter of little gray foxes. And later
A litter of little white foxes.
The white ones are lighter than gray. Not a lot.
The gray ones are lighter than black. Just a little.
The litters are lighter in moonlight. They glitter.
They gleam in the moonlight. They glow and they glisten.
Out on the snow see the silver fox sparkle.

CAN YOU COPY?

The okapi is shy and high-strung;
She stays with her mate and her young;
I've heard that she hears
Rather well with her ears
And she washes her eyes with her tongue.

She washes her eyes with her *tongue?*
Yes, she washes her eyes with her tongue:
It is long; it is floppy;
And thus the okapi
Can wash out her eyes with her tongue.

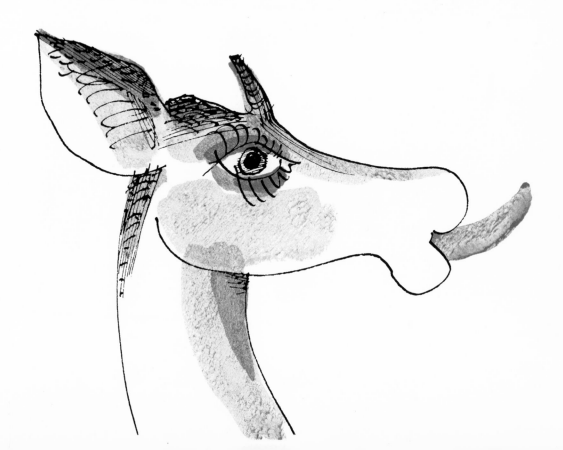

ADVICE

If you're sleepy in the jungle
And you wish to find a pillow,
Take a friendly word of warning:
DO NOT USE AN ARMADILLO!

Though an armadillo often
May roll up just like a pillow,
Do not go by his appearance
But go by with ample clearance.

For an armadillo's armor
Is not suited for a pillow,
And an armadillo's temper
Only suits an armadillo.

If you use him for a pillow,
Then beware of what will follow:
He may slip out while you're sleeping
And an arm or two he'll swallow.

    (And any beast that leaves you armless
    Can't be classified as harmless!)

Nor will he beg your pardon
For his thoughtless peccadillo;
So the next time you go walking in the jungle
TAKE A PILLOW!

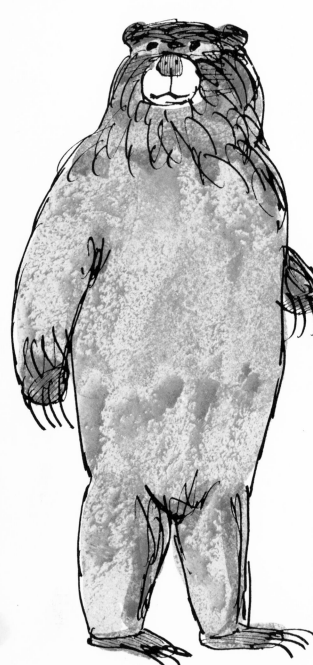

BEAR

I like to watch the big bear walk
When I go to the zoo;
Sometimes
Four feet
Seem
Two
Too
Much
And up he goes on two.

Then after he has strolled about
And roared an awful roar,
Sometimes
Two feet
Seem
Two
Too
Few
And down he goes on four.

RHINOCEROS

I often wonder whether
The rhinoceros's leather
Is as bumpy on the inside
As it is upon the skinside.

BACKWARD RUNNING PORCUPINES

Backward running porcupines

are angry mean and quick.

Meeting one behind, before,

beware, be off, don't stick

Around or you get stuck. Bad luck.

So cover ground, my friend

For if you do not get away

you get it in the end.

PANDA

A panda
Planned a visit
But they told him not to come.
He was going to Uganda
(Where of course he isn't from).
Everybody knows the panda
Comes from China not Uganda
And a
Panda
In Uganda
Would cause panda-monium.

STORK STORY

White storks spend their winters
In Africa
       and
India

White storks spend their summers
In Holland
       and
In Germany

White storks do their nesting
On rooftops
       and
On chimney tops
In Holland
       and
In Germany

White storks hatch their babies
From eggs they lay
In nests they build
On rooftops
       and
On chimney tops
In Holland
       and
In Germany

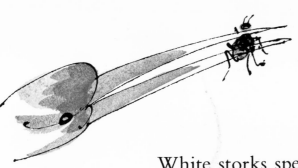

White storks spend their summers
Catching slugs
And birds
And bugs
To feed their hungry babies
Who hatch from eggs
In nests they build
On rooftops
        and
On chimney tops
In Holland
        and
In Germany

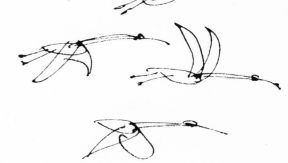

Then in the autumn weather
They all fly off together
To spend another winter
In Africa
        and
India

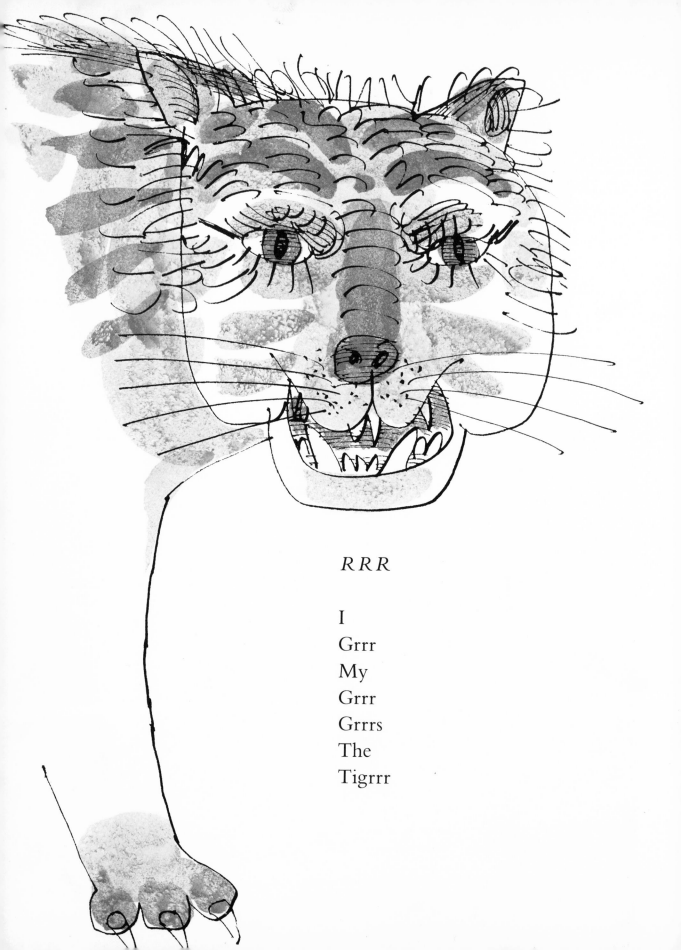

RRR

I
Grrr
My
Grrr
Grrrs
The
Tigrrr

WALRUS

The walrus often weighs a ton,
And though he's not considered fat,
To weigh a ton cannot be fun.
                Can you imagine weighing that?

He only knows the icy floes,
The Arctic snows spread everywhere,
The bitter breeze, the freezing seas.
                Can you imagine living there?

And when he's hungry for a meal,
What does he do, do you suppose?
He digs up mollusks with his tusks.
                Can you imagine eating those?

The walrus lives on frozen shores.
The walrus loves to dive and swim.
His life is not like mine or yours.
                Can you imagine being him?

GAZELLE

O gaze on the graceful gazelle as it grazes
It grazes on green growing leaves and on grasses
On grasses it grazes, go gaze as it passes
It passes so gracefully, gently, O gaze!

WHAT'S THEIR NAME?

In Africa
There lives a bird
Whose name contains
A certain word.

A badger also
Has this name.
Each of them
Is named the same.

Both are named
For what they eat:
Something sticky,
Something sweet

Manufactured
By a bee
Named the same
So that makes three!

_____ bird
Hunts out the nest.
What's inside it?
Have you guessed?

_____ badger
Does arrive.
Steals the _____
From the hive.

_____bee
Begins to sting.
Badger hardly
Feels a thing,

Feasts on _____
With the bird.
Bee is angry!
What's the word?

ANTEATER

The anteater
The anteater
It hasn't any teeth
    Neither in the jaw above
    Nor in the jaw beneath.

The anteater
The anteater
It hardly has a jaw
    Without a jaw
    Without some teeth
    It cannot chew or gnaw.

    Its tongue is long and sticky.
    Its snout is long and thin.
    Its mouth is very little
    So little food fits in.

    With such an apparatus
    It can't eat meat or plants.
    No plants? No meat?
    What *can* it eat?
The anteater
Eats

SLOTH

A tree's a trapeze for a sloth.
He clings with his claws to its growth.
    Both the sloth and his wife
    Lead an upside-down life.
To lead such a life I'd be loath.

LION

Look!
A lion!
Mighty beast.

       (Might he
       Bite me
       For a feast?)

Though
I know
He wouldn't dare,

       I'm mighty glad

he's over there.

TARANTULA

Ta ran! Ta ra!
Tarantula!
    A spider big and hairy!
Its bite might frighten you a bit,
    And I admit it's scary.
In Italy, if you get bit,
    You whirl around pell-mell, a
Bit like being in a fit. . . .
    And *that's* the tarantella!

OCELOT

The ocelot's a clever cat.
She knowsalot of this and that.
She growsalot of spotted fur
Which looks extremely well on her.

In places where it snowsalot
She seldom ever goesalot.
She much prefers it where it's hot.
That's all about the ocelot.

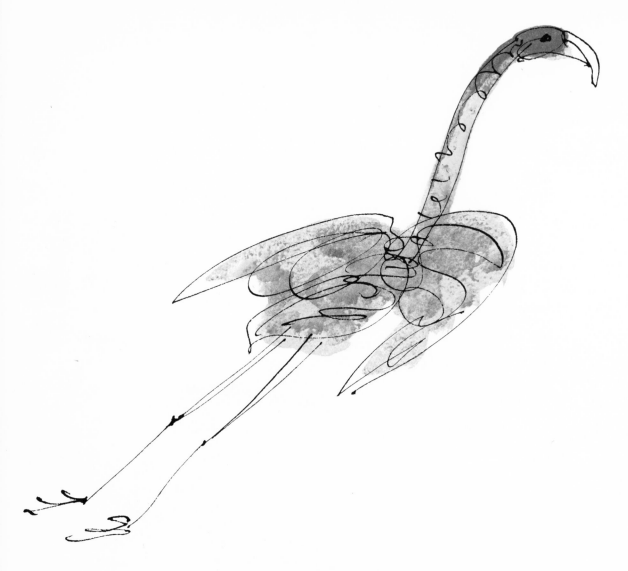

FLAMINGO

Sea risen sunbird
O flaming flamingo, spread
Wide your red feathers.

ELEPHANT

The elephant's a bulky beast;
He weighs a thousand pounds at least;
And what to you would be a feast
    Is not a filler-upper
To him. All day he has to hunch
Above his trough and munch and munch
And by the time he's done with lunch
    It's time to start on supper.

WISH

I'd like to be
A kangaroo
And have a pocket
Made of me.

TAPIR

The tapir has a tubby torse.
He is not very big.
Although related to the horse,
He looks more like a pig.

If I were in the tapir's shoes
(Although I'm not of course),
Relation to the pig I'd choose,
Resemblance to the horse.

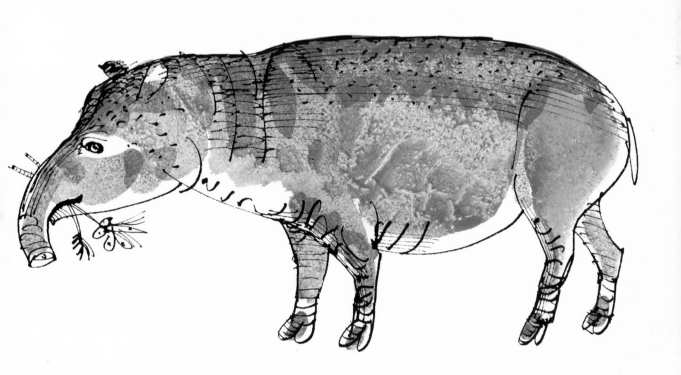

PENGUIN

O Penguin, do you ever try
To flap your flipper wings and fly?
How do you feel, a bird by birth
And yet for life tied down to earth?
A feathered creature, born with wings
Yet never wingborne. All your kings
And emperors must wonder why
Their realm is sea instead of sky.

HIPPOPOTAMUS

Pygmy hippopota-
Muses have not got a
Lot of hair

Anywhere.

ANTHROPOIDS

The next time you go to the zoo
The zoo
Slow down for a minute or two
Or two
     And consider the apes,
     All their sizes and shapes,
For they all are related to you
To you.

Yes, they all are related to you
To you
And they all are related to me
To me
     To our fathers and mothers,
     Our sisters and brothers
And all of the people we see
We see.

The chimpanzees, gorillas, and all
And all
The orangutans climbing the wall
The wall
        These remarkable creatures
        Share most of our features
And the difference between us is small
Quite small.

So the next time you go to the zoo
The zoo
Slow down for a minute or two
Or two
    And consider the apes,
    All their sizes and shapes,
For they all are related to you
To you.

ABOUT THE AUTHOR

MARY ANN HOBERMAN was born and grew up in Stamford, Connecticut, and was graduated from Smith College. She lives in Greenwich, Connecticut, with her husband Norman, who is an architect, and their four children. When not writing children's books, Mrs. Hoberman gardens, plays tennis, and performs with The Pocket People, a children's theater group which she helped found several years ago.

Writing poetry, especially for children, is one of her favorite occupations. "*Not* writing a poem would be more difficult. An odd fact or the sound of a name catches my ear or, more likely, its rhythm catches my feet; it irritates me as a grain of sand irritates an oyster; I can't get rid of it. Slowly it accretes related words and images until finally it is not a pearl but a poem. And only then can I be free of it and turn my attention to something else. Usually another poem."

ABOUT THE ILLUSTRATOR

As a young man JOSEPH LOW studied at the Art Students' League, taught briefly at Indiana University, then moved to Connecticut where he began to illustrate books, founded a private press, and developed a passion for sailing. His prints and the publications of his Eden Hill Press are to be found in museums and private collections both here and abroad. He and his wife now divide their year between Martha's Vineyard in the summer and the Virgin Islands in the winter: both excellent sailing waters.